W9-CRX-077

ANIMAL MECHANICALS

Reptiles

Tom Jackson

PowerKiDS
press

Published in 2017 by
The Rosen Publishing Group, Inc.
29 East 21st Street, New York, NY 10010

Cataloging-in-Publication Data

Names: Jackson, Tom.
Title: Reptiles / Tom Jackson.
Description: New York : PowerKids Press, 2017. | Series: Animal mechanicals | Includes index.
Identifiers: ISBN 9781499422504 (pbk.) | ISBN 9781508150268 (library bound) | ISBN 9781508150145 (6 pack)
Subjects: LCSH: Reptiles--Juvenile literature.
Classification: LCC QL644.2 J32 2017 | DDC 597.9--dc23

Copyright © 2017 Brown Bear Books Ltd

For Brown Bear Books Ltd:
Editorial Director: Lindsey Lowe
Editor: Tom Jackson
Children's Publisher: Anne O'Daly
Design Manager: Keith Davis
Designer: Lynne Lennon
Picture Manager: Sophie Mortimer

Picture Credits
T=Top, C=Center, B=Bottom, L=Left, R=Right
Front Cover: 1st swatch, ©Shutterstock/Coffee Lover; 2nd swatch, ©Shutterstock/tratong; 3rd swatch, ©Shutterstock/ Aleksandar Mijatovic; python, ©Shutterstock/Eric Isselee; chameleon tail, ©Shutterstock/Mark Bridger; crocodile, ©Shutterstock/nattanan726 / Shutterstock; thorny devil, ©Shutterstock/Kristian Bell / Shutterstock; frilled lizard, ©Shutterstock/Matt Cornish / Shutterstock; snake skeleton illustration, ©Shutterstock/Leremy; push pins, ©Shutterstock/ Picsfive / Shutterstock; lined paper, ©Shutterstock/Yuttasak Jannarong. **Inside:** 1, ©Shutterstock/K Kaplin; 4cl, ©Thinkstock/ iStock; 4bl, ©Thinkstock/A Dogs Life/iStock; 4br, ©Dreamstime/I Dream Photos; 5, ©Thinkstock/A Dogs Life/iStock; 6-7t, ©Shutterstock/Audrey Snider-Bell; 6-7b, ©Shutterstock/Heiki Kiera; 7, ©Shutterstock/Funny Angel; 8-9, ©Shutterstock/ Hin255; 9tr, ©Shutterstock/Ryan M. Bolton; 9cr, ©Shutterstock/Nico99; 10-11, ©Dreamstime/Lukas Blazek; 11, ©Shutterstock/ Reptiles 4 All; 12t, ©Shutterstock/Reptiles 4 All; 12b, ©Shutterstock/Cathy Keifer; 13cl, ©Shutterstock/Reptiles 4 All; 13cr, ©Shutterstock/Reptiles 4 All; 14, ©Shutterstock/Bildagentur GmbH; 15tr, ©Shutterstock/G. Tipene; 15c, ©Shutterstock/K Kaplin; 16-17, ©Shutterstock/Bildagentur GmbH; 17c, ©Shutterstock/Neal Cooper; 17b, ©Shutterstock/Stuart G. Porter; 18-19, ©Shutterstock/Richard Susanto; 19c, ©Shutterstock/Luca Vaime; 20-21, ©Shutterstock/Smileus; 21, ©Thinkstock/African Way/iStock; 22-23c, ©Thinkstock/Milan Vaslcek/Hemera; 22-23b, ©Dreamstime/K M Lauer; 23, ©Shutterstock/Hecke61; 24, ©Thinkstock/John Carriemolia/iStock; 24-25, ©Shutterstock/Janelle Lugge; 26b, ©Dreamstime/Carla F Castango; 26-27c, ©Shutterstock/Christian Scholissingeyer; 27, ©Shutterstock/Ethan Daniels; 28cl, ©Shutterstock/Reptiles 4 All; 28cr, ©Shutterstock/Mattia ATH; 28b, ©Shutterstock/Praisaeng; 29cl, ©Shutterstock/Richard Susanto; 29cr, ©Shutterstock/ Lipowski Milas; 29b, ©Thinkstock/A Kuzmik/iStock.

Brown Bear Books has made every attempt to contact the copyright holder.
If anyone has any information please contact licensing@brownbearbooks.co.uk

All rights reserved. No part of this book may be reproduced in any form
without permission in writing from the publisher, except by a reviewer.

Manufactured in the United States of America

CPSIA Compliance Information: Batch #BS16PK: For Further Information contact Rosen Publishing, New York, New York at 1-800-237-9932

CONTENTS

Reptile Machines

There are some machines that can see using heat, walk on ceilings, change color completely, and gather drinking water from the air.

These machines are called reptiles. A reptile body is a living machine. It is equipped with moving parts, sensors, and a power supply, just like any mechanical machine. The reptile body makes use of different designs to survive in different ways. For example, turtle and crocodile bodies are armored with plates of bone; snakes have no legs so they can slither into small spaces in search of food; and lizard skin can be used for communication.

Crocodilian: Caiman

Snake: Palm viper

The Four Main Reptile Groups:

CROCODILIAN	✳	Large hunters that live in water
TURTLE	✳	Mostly plant-eaters that are protected by a shell
SNAKE	✳	Legless hunters that kill with venom or by squeezing their prey to death
LIZARD	✳	Most have four legs and a long tail

Turtle: Green sea turtle

Reptile Tech Spec

There are more than 10,000 different kinds of reptile. They live all over the world, even in the oceans, but are most common in places with warm weather. Most reptiles lay eggs covered in a waterproof shell, but some give birth to their young. Reptile bodies are built in many different ways to suit the places they live in, but they all share two basic characteristics:

* The skin is covered in scales, which are made of keratin, a waxy, waterproof substance that is also used to make the claws. (Feathers and hairs are also made of keratin.)

* The animal's body temperature is the same as the surroundings. This is known as being "cold-blooded."

Lizard:
Blue iguana

Eyes have good color vision and can see ultraviolet light.

Skin is green-gray to blend in with rocks; becomes bluer during mating season.

Long claws used to grip when climbing in trees and for digging nests and burrows.

At 5 feet (1.5 m) long and weighing 30 pounds (14 kg), the blue iguana from the Cayman Islands is the largest lizard living in the Americas.

Snake

VENOM DELIVERY

If you designed a machine that killed its prey in seconds and could work almost anywhere, what would you come up with?

Diamond-shaped marks along the body.

Rattle, made of loose scales.

FACT FILE

Common name: Western diamondback rattlesnake

Length: 30 in (76 cm) to 7 ft (2.1 m)

Appearance: gray or brown skin with large diamond markings

Where they live: North America

Habitat: desert, semidesert, and dry grasslands

Prey: small mammals, birds

Predators: hawks, weasels, king snakes, humans

Fangs fold out from roof of mouth before snake bites.

KILLER MENU

The Western diamondback is North America's most dangerous snake. More people die from bites of this snake than any other. The snake identifies its prey and then attacks with powerful poison.

HEAT SENSOR	Two heat-sensitive pits near the eyes detect prey, even in darkness
VENOM	Attacks the victim's blood vessels, making them burst; victim bleeds internally until it becomes unconscious or dies

BIOMIMIC:

A rattlesnake's mouth is a venom injection system. The two fangs are hollow, and when they bite, they create a channel for venom to enter the victim's body. A hypodermic needle works in the same way.

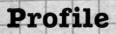

Profile

The rattle is unique to rattlesnakes. It is made of keratin, the same material that makes claws and hair. The snake shakes the rattle in the air as a defense, to warn large animals not to step on it.

Gecko

A tough, off-road SUV can go most places, but even it cannot go straight up a wall. To do that, you'll need to use a gecko's design.

STICKY FEET

FACT FILE

Common name: Gecko

Length: 1.2–14 in (3–36 cm)

Weight: 0.004–7.1 oz (0.1–200 g)

Color: mostly green or brown but many have spotted and striped patterns of reds, blues, and yellows

Where it lives: wherever it is warm all year around; most common in forests and rocky deserts; several species live inside homes

Prey: insects and spiders

Predators: birds, rats, cats, and snakes

Padded toes can stick to any surface allowing the gecko to walk up walls and even upside down across ceilings.

Used as a fifth limb to push the body upward while climbing.

BIOMIMIC:

A gecko's toe pads can grip anything, but they do not use sticky liquid like glue. Engineers have copied the fine folding structure of the pads to make superstrong grippers. A strip the size of a bankcard can hold the weight of three people.

Profile

There are at least 1,600 species of gecko living in the warm parts of the world. They are little hunters that are most active at night as they scurry around looking for bugs. Geckos have large eyes to see in the dark, but no eyelids to keep them clean. However, the gecko's tongue is long enough to wash its eyes with a single lick.

Skin can change color, becoming paler and brighter during the night.

Toe pads have folds with skin covered in tiny hairlike flaps that grip any surface.

CLIMBING EQUIPMENT

TONGUE	Long and sticky for grabbing prey
CLAWS	On toes along with pads to add extra grip on loose surfaces
EYE	Is 350 times more sensitive to color than human eyes in some species
SKIN	Outer layer shed at once every three or four weeks to remove dirt and damage
TAIL	Falls off if grabbed; new one grows in its place in some species

Alligator Snapping Turtle

TRICKING PREY

This body design combines a stealth mode with a powerful bite strength and tough defenses. It also uses a trick to lure target prey.

WEAPONS SYSTEM

The alligator snapping turtle is an ambush hunter that lies in wait on the riverbed. Once prey is close, the turtle strikes with lightning speed. However, it is also well defended from attack.

CLAWS	Long and hooked on all four feet, used for gripping riverbed, digging, and fighting
SPINES	On the tail and throat make it hard for predators to hold turtle
SLIME	Algae grows on the surface of shell making it green and better camouflaged

Named for alligators because the spikes on the shell look like an alligator's armor.

TECH SPECS

When prey is in striking distance, the turtle uses a vacuum effect to suck it toward its mouth. The turtle opens its mouth very fast. Water rushes in, and that pulls the prey with it.

* Holds breath for 50 minutes at a time

Profile

The alligator snapping turtle is the largest river turtle in North America. It spends most of its time lurking on the muddy river bottom in murky water that is 6 to 12 feet (1.8 to 3.7 m) deep. Only the females leave the river. They move up to 160 feet (50 m) inland to find dry soil in which to bury their eggs.

Tip of the tongue is bright red and stands out in the dark water. Fish and other prey mistake it for a worm and swim right into the turtle's mouth.

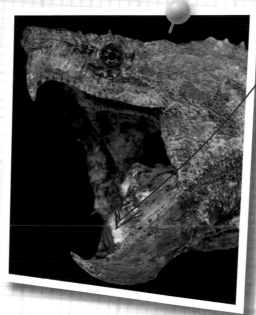

Sharp beak strong enough to cut through a person's finger. Hooked tips used to grab hold of larger prey.

FACT FILE

Common name: Alligator snapping turtle

Length: 26 in (66 cm)

Weight: 176 lbs (80 kg)

Color: brown and yellow, but the shell is often covered in green algae

Where it lives: in the slow-flowing rivers and swamps of the eastern United States

Food: fish, frogs, worms, and snakes

Predators: no natural predators but threatened by human pet traders who gather young turtles from the wild

Chameleon

CHANGING COLOR

Having skin that can change color is a useful design feature for staying out of sight. It is also useful for communication.

FACT FILE

Common name: Chameleon

Length: 1.2–27 in (3–68.5 cm)

Weight: 0.007 oz–1.5 lbs (0.2–680 g)

Color: mostly green to blend in with leafy habitat but able to turn skin almost any color, including red, yellow, orange, and blue

Where it lives: forests, woodlands, and grasslands of Africa, south Asia, and southern Europe

Prey: insects, spiders, frogs, small birds, and small mammals

Predators: eagles, cats, and snakes

Skin is normally pale green to help the lizard stay hidden among the leaves.

Profile

There are about 200 species of chameleon, mostly living in the forests of Africa. They hunt for insects during the day, moving very slowly so they don't disturb their prey. A few chameleons give birth to young, but most lay eggs, burying them in soil. The eggs take several months to hatch, with one species taking two years!

TECH SPECS

A chameleon's skin contains yellow pigments. This is usually mixed with blue light that reflects off a layer of tiny crystals underneath, making the skin green. To change color, the lizard rearranges the crystals so they reflect other colors instead of blue.

FAULT FINDER

Chameleons have no opening to let sound into their inner ear. Although they can hear, they can only pick up a small range of sounds.

Skin changes into bright pattern to communicate with other chameleons.

The colors show the lizard's mood, such as angry or relaxed.

HUNTING SYSTEM

TOES	Work like pairs of pincers to grip branches
EYES	Can move independently and look in two directions at once, so lizard can scan for prey
TONGUE	Almost twice as long as the body (not including the tail); when it hits the target, the tip forms a sucker that holds the prey

Frilled Lizard

This lizard uses shock tactics. It has a hidden body mechanism that transforms it into what appears to be a larger and fiercer animal.

WARNING SIGNS

FACT FILE

Common name: Frilled lizard

Length: 3 ft (0.9 m)

Weight: 1.1 lbs (0.5 kg)

Color: brown, yellow, and gray with brighter oranges and reds that are shown when frill is opened

Where it lives: in the dry forests of Australia and New Guinea where there are large clearings between the trees

Prey: ants, spiders, cicadas, other insects, and small vertebrates

Predators: birds of prey, snakes, and dingoes

Most of the time frill of skin is folded flat over the neck.

FAULT FINDER

The frilled lizard has to sunbathe in the morning to warm up its body. While it is still cold, it does not have the energy to escape predators.

 ## BIOMIMIC:

The lizard's frill is not just an escape system. It is also opened when the lizard needs to release unwanted heat. The International Space Station has long, flat radiators that stick out into space to do the same job.

Profile

Frilled lizards spend most of their time in trees, where they prey on insects and spiders. They climb down to the ground to escape tree snakes and attacking birds. They also cross open areas to search for ant nests to raid and to hunt for larger prey. This is when they may use the frill.

Frill contains spines of cartilage; spines are raised to unfold a large flap of colorful skin. That makes the lizard look much bigger and fiercer.

Lizard also jumps and opens mouth very wide to startle predator.

ESCAPE PLAN

The lizard does not rely only on its frill to scare away predators. It also has other ways of escaping attacks.

GUMS	Inside of mouth is pale compared to the lizard's skin; that adds to the shocking effect when the mouth gapes open
RUNS	After flapping frill, lizard turns around and runs on back legs in opposite direction—keeping the frill on show
CLIMBS	Heads for tree and uses claws to run up trunk to finally get away from attacker

Crocodile

BIG BITE

This monster's jaws are built to crush with awesome power.

FACT FILE

Common name: Nile crocodile

Length: 16 ft (5 m)

Weight: 1,540 lbs (700 kg)

Color: yellow, black, and brown when young but becomes dull gray-green as algae grow on skin of older animals

Where it lives: rivers of Africa

Prey: fish, antelopes, and birds

Predators: no natural predators

Huge muscles close the jaw; the ones that open it are much weaker.

Cone-shaped teeth dig into prey so they cannot wriggle free from bite.

WATER HUNTER

Nile crocodiles ambush prey from shallow water. These features make them deadly predators.

EYES	On top of head so above water when rest of body is submerged; see-through eyelid protects eye underwater
NOSTRILS	Close when crocodile is underwater
ENERGY	Body is very efficient so a big crocodile can survive on one large meal a year

Crocodile opens its mouth to cool down on hot days.

TECH SPECS

The Nile crocodile's long jaws work like a huge pair of pincers. The force of this crocodile's bite is more powerful than that of any other animal, including the great white shark, tiger, and killer whale!

Crocodiles cannot chew food; instead they swallow chunks whole.

A valve shuts the windpipe and throat so that water does not flood in when the mouth is open underwater.

Profile

The Nile crocodile is the largest reptile in Africa. Like most crocodiles and alligators, it hunts close to the water's edge, waiting there for prey to come close. Then it strikes at great speed, lunging forward and grabbing prey in its jaws. Large prey are usually pulled into the water where they drown.

Komodo Dragon

This giant lizard does not rely just on its strength and speed to kill prey. It uses a venomous bite that kills its victims slowly but surely.

MIGHTY HUNTER

FACT FILE

Common name: Komodo dragon

Length: 10 ft (3 m)

Weight: 330 lbs (150 kg)

Color: black and gray

Where it lives: the forested islands of Komodo, Flores, and Rinca plus a few smaller islets in eastern Indonesia

Prey: cattle, donkeys, deer, pigs, and carrion (the remains of dead animals)

Predators: no natural predators, but the giant lizards have been cleared from many islands by humans

Claws used for climbing, digging burrows, and as weapons in fights with other dragons.

Profile

The Komodo dragon is the largest lizard in the world. It lives on a few islands in Indonesia. The lizard evolved from a much smaller ancestor, like lizards that live in other places. However, the islands had no other predators, so the Komodo dragon evolved to be a giant hunter.

FAULT FINDER

Fully grown Komodo dragons prey on younger ones. To avoid these cannibals, small dragons climb trees, where the bigger lizards cannot reach them.

Rounded scales are armored with plates of bone. Each scale is sensitive to touch.

TECH SPECS
The Komodo dragon's venom takes hours or even days to work. The dragon trails its victim while the venom works and weakens its heart. Eventually the prey dies.

Nose can smell dead body from 6 miles (10 km) away.

Long forked tongue picks up the scent of prey.

Venom is mixed into the dragon's thick, sticky saliva and enters the victim's blood when the lizard bites.

GIANT KILLER

TAIL	Used to balance the lizard as it stands on its back legs; lizard does this during wrestling fights with rivals
TEETH	Small with sawlike edges to draw blood during bites
LEGS	Stick out sideways and hold the body close to the ground; lizard mostly walks slowly but is capable of burst of high-speed running

Giant Tortoise

This machine cannot outrun attackers because it hauls heavy armor around with it. However, that armor ensures survival from most attacks.

FULLY ARMORED

FACT FILE

Common name: Galápagos tortoise

Length: 4 ft (1.2 m)

Weight: 475 lbs (215 kg)

Color: pale brown, gray, and black

Where it lives: on the Galapagos Islands in the Pacific Ocean, which are covered in dry forests and shrubs

Food: grasses, leaves, and cacti

Predators: no natural predators on the islands but sailors used to load living tortoises on ships as a source of food on long voyages; the tortoises are now in danger of extinction

Domed section covers the back while a flat plate protects the belly.

Plates have a waterproof covering made of keratin.

Shell made of plates of bone that are attached to the tortoise's ribs.

SLOW BUT SURE

SENSES	Hearing is very poor and the tortoise relies more on its eyes and nose to move about and search for food
SHAPE	Shell design varies according to habitat; grass-eaters have rounded shells while leaf-eaters have saddle-shaped shells
BLADDER	Stores water so tortoise does not have to drink for up to 18 months

Ancient Roman soldiers used a special defense to protect themselves from arrows. The soldiers formed a square. Those on the edges made a wall with their shields; the men in the middle held their shields above their heads to make a roof. The formation was called the *testudo,* which is Latin for "tortoise."

Profile

Giant tortoises only live on a few islands far out to sea. The most famous is the Galápagos tortoise. The Aldabra tortoise (below) from the Seychelles in the Indian Ocean is slightly larger, with some weighing 550 pounds (250 kg). Both tortoises can live for more than 100 years.

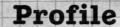

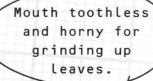

Mouth toothless and horny for grinding up leaves.

Large, dark scales on the legs protect the skin from strong sunlight.

Front feet are turned inward making it easier for the tortoise to carry the heavy shell.

FAULT FINDER

The tortoise cannot walk in straight lines but sways from side to side at the very low speed of 0.2 mph (0.3 km/h).

Gharial

FISH CATCHER

What are the components needed to make an expert fisher? The gharial's design has them all.

FACT FILE

Common name: Gharial

Length: 11–20 feet (3.5–6 m)

Weight: 200–350 lbs (90–160 kg)

Color: gray-green and yellow but grow darker with age

Where it lives: in the river systems of India, Pakistan, and Bangladesh

Prey: mostly fish

Predators: no natural predators, although the gharial is now rare because many of the sandbanks where it rests have been removed by people

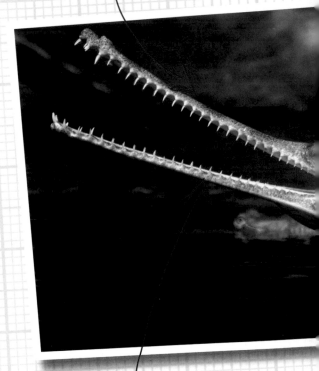

Small, pointed teeth grip slippery prey.

The narrow jaws are four times longer than they are wide; they sweep side to side through water to snatch fish.

TECH SPECS

The gharial's snout is narrow so it does not cause drag as it swings through the water. Any fish that pass between the jaws are grabbed by the pointed teeth and cannot escape.

UNDERWATER HUNTER

Although it is a relative of the crocodile, the gharial does not attack land animals. It only catches small swimming animals and has special features to help it do that.

FEET	Webbed so they work as paddles for swimming in deep water
TAIL CREST	Flattened spines along tail make it work like an oar when swung from side to side
LIPS	Jaw cannot fully close and teeth form spiky layer between the lips
LEGS	Short and cannot lift the body; animal slithers over land on its belly

Males have round "pot" on snout for making calls underwater.

Skin-covered bone plates protect the back.

Profile

The gharial lives in the rivers of South Asia. It lives in large groups that gather on sandbanks in the middle of wide waterways to sunbathe between hunts. Although it is not as heavy and powerful as a large crocodile, the gharial is about the same length as the saltwater crocodile, the largest reptile on Earth today.

Thorny Devil

Living in a desert is hard unless you can find water. This little lizard has a body design that lets it collect its own supply of drinking water.

WATER COLLECTOR

Profile

The thorny devil is an ant-eating lizard. It searches for the trails the ants use and then follows them, licking up the insects with its short tongue. The lizard can eat 3,000 ants in one go. Living out in the open is risky, and the thorny devil is covered in prickles to fend off attackers.

Walks with tail up to knock droplets of dew off surrounding plants.

DESERT SURVIVAL

GROOVES	Water is drawn through grooves by capillary action, the same process that sucks water into a sponge
MOUTH	Opens and closes to suck in water and pull more toward the head along the skin grooves
WALK	Sways from side to side as it walks; this matches the movements of the dried leaves that cover the ground where the lizard hunts

BIOMIMIC:

Thorny devils collect water from the air. The water vapor turns into liquid droplets on the skin. Humans have developed a self-filling water bottle that collects water in the same way.

FAULT FINDER

The thorny devil cannot hunt when it gets cold. In the winter, it digs a burrow to stay warm and waits until the weather is warmer.

Spiked lump on the neck is a false head that fools predators.

When attacked, lizard tucks real head between its legs; predator bites false head and causes less damage.

Dew forms on the prickly spikes on the body; water flows through grooves on the skin to the mouth.

FACT FILE

Common name: Thorny devil

Length: 8 in (20 cm)

Weight: 3.4 oz (95 g)

Color: brown and orange to match the reddish sands and leaves

Where it lives: the deserts of Australia

Prey: ants—can eat up to 3,000 in one meal

Predators: falcons and other ground-hunting birds of prey

Python

HEAT SEEKER

This amazing hunter is armed with a super sense. It can detect prey even in the dark and kills with a powerful squeeze.

FACT FILE

Common name: Python

Length: 20 in–23 ft (50 cm–7 m)

Weight: 0.5–130 lbs (0.2–59 kg)

Color: mostly brown, green, and yellow in striped and blotchy patterns; some are bright green or yellow

Where it lives: Africa, Asia, and Australia in forests, deserts, and grasslands

Prey: birds and mammals

Predators: young eaten by birds

The upper and lower jaw have an elastic link so they can open wide enough to swallow large prey whole.

BIOMIMIC:

The python's heat-sensitive pits work in the same way as an infrared camera. These cameras convert the heat of an object, like this cat, into a colored picture we can see.

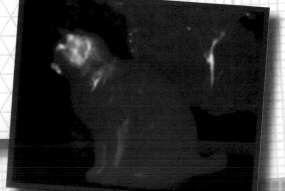

The snake's pupil is a vertical slit. That means it is good at seeing up-and-down motions but less able to spot things moving from side to side.

Profile

There are about 25 species of python. The anthill python is the smallest at less than 2 feet (60 cm), but most pythons are large snakes. The Burmese python (pictured) is 19 feet (5.8 m) long, while the reticulated python is the longest snake of all at 23 feet (7 m) long.

Hollow pits on snout are sensitive to heat so the python can detect warm-blooded prey in the dark.

Tongue smells as well as tastes. It collects odors from the air and feeds them into a smelling organ in the roof of the mouth.

HUNTING MACHINE

TEETH	Curved backward so when prey struggles in the mouth, the teeth dig deeper in, making it impossible for the prey to escape
TONGUE	Forked to help pinpoint direction of smells when one side of tongue picks up more odor than the other
COILS	Prey squeezed by python's coiled body, making it impossible for the prey to breathe

MECHANICALS QUIZ

Now that you know more, test your knowledge of reptiles with this fun quiz. Answers on page 32.

1 True or false: A snake's tongue is used for smelling as well as tasting.

2 Where do giant tortoises live?

3 How long can a crocodile go without eating?

REPTILE RECORDS

BIGGEST	Saltwater crocodile 23 ft (7 m); 2.2 tons (2 tonnes)
SMALLEST	Jaragua sphaero (dwarf gecko) 1.2 in (3 cm)
LARGEST LIZARD	Komodo dragon 10 ft (3 m); 330 lbs (150 kg)
LARGEST SNAKE	Green anaconda 17 ft (5.2 m); 215 lbs (97.5 kg)
LARGEST TURTLE	Leatherback 7 ft (2.1 m); 1,433 lbs (650 kg)
TOP RUNNER	Bearded dragon 25 mph (40 km/h)
TOP SWIMMER	Leatherback 22 mph (35 km/h)
LONGEST LIFE	Galápagos tortoise 170 years (100 years in wild)
DEADLIEST	Indian cobra bites kill 12,000 people each year

4 Is a Komodo dragon venomous?

5 Why do chameleons change color?

BIOMIMIC:

Some reptiles have three eyes. The third one is hidden under the skin on the top of the head. Known as the parietal eye, it does not make images but can detect the brightness of light. A light detector (pictured) on a camera does the same thing to indicate whether to use the flash or not.

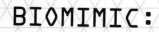

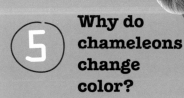

29

Glossary

algae Microscopic plant-like organisms that use photosynthesis to make food.

biomimic To copy the design of a living body to make a machine.

cannibal An animal that eats members of its own species.

cartilage A bendy substance used in the skeleton; cartilage is strong but more flexible than bone.

component A part of a larger unit.

elastic Able to change shape when pulled but always returns to its original shape.

hypodermic Under the skin.

infrared Producing or using rays of invisible light that are longer than rays that produce red light.

keratin A waxy protein that is used to make many animal body parts, such as hairs and feathers.

ligament A cord that connects bones together at joints.

odor A smell.

pigment A colored chemical inside living things.

predator An animal that hunts other animals for food.

prey An animal that is hunted by another animal.

pupil The dark center of the eye where the light comes in.

radiator A panel or similar object that gives out heat.

semidesert An area that is dry for much of the year but receives a little more rain than a desert.

species A group of animals or plants that look very similar and are able to breed and have young.

ultraviolet An invisible form of light that comes from the sun; ultraviolet creates sunburns and suntans.

valve A device that opens and closes a tube or pipe.

venom A poison that is injected into a body by an animal.

vertical Upright.

waterproof Describing a barrier that stops water soaking through.

water vapor The gas form of water that is present in the air.

windpipe The tube that carries the air from the mouth and nose to the lungs.

Further Information

Books

Alderton, David. *Snakes and Reptiles Around the World.* Mankato, MN: Smart Apple Media, 2015.

Gagne, Tammy. *Snakes: Built for the Hunt.* North Mankato, MN: Capstone Press, 2016.

Herrington, Lisa M. *Remarkable Reptiles.* New York: Children's Press, 2016.

Kratt, Martin. *Wild Reptiles: Snakes, Crocodiles, Lizards, and Turtles!* New York: Random House, 2015.

Lewis, Clare. *Reptile Body Parts.* Chicago, IL: Capstone Heinemann Library, 2016.

Linde, Barbara M. 20 *Fun Facts about Reptile Adaptations.* New York: Gareth Stevens Publishing, 2016.

Websites

PowerKids Press has developed an online list of websites related to the subject of this book. This site is updated regularly. Please use this link to access the list:

www.powerkidslinks.com/am/reptiles

Index

Answers to the Quiz:

1. True
2. Galápagos Islands and the Seychelles
3. Only needs to eat once a year

4. Yes, venom is mixed into the saliva
5. Mostly to communicate with other
   lizards